ONCE UPON A BEDTIME
A Collection of Stories for Sharing

LITTLE TIGER PRESS
An imprint of Magi Publications
1 The Coda Centre, 189 Munster Road,
London SW6 6AW
www.littletigerpress.com

First published in Great Britain 2009
This volume copyright
© Magi Publications 2009
Cover illustration copyright
© Tim Warnes 2006

THE VERY SLEEPY SLOTH
Andrew Murray
Illustrated by Jack Tickle
First published in Great Britain 2003
by Little Tiger Press
An imprint of Magi Publications
Text copyright © Andrew Murray 2003
Illustrations copyright © Jack Tickle 2003

THE SMALLEST BEAR
Anne Mangan
Illustrated by Joanne Moss
First published in Great Britain 1998
by Little Tiger Press
An imprint of Magi Publications
Text copyright © Anne Mangan 1998
Illustrations copyright © Joanne Moss 1998

IT COULD HAVE BEEN WORSE . . .
A. H. Benjamin
Illustrated by Tim Warnes
First published in Great Britain 1998
by Little Tiger Press
An imprint of Magi Publications
Text copyright © A. H. Benjamin 1998
Illustrations copyright © Tim Warnes 1998

OUCH!
Ragnhild Scamell
Illustrated by Michael Terry
First published in Great Britain 2006
by Little Tiger Press
An imprint of Magi Publications
Text copyright © Ragnhild Scamell 2006
Illustrations copyright © Michael Terry 2006

Once Upon a Bedtime

A Collection of Stories for Sharing

LITTLE TIGER PRESS

London

Contents

IT COULD HAVE BEEN WORSE . . .
A. H. Benjamin & Tim Warnes

OUCH!
Ragnhild Scamell & Michael Terry

Andrew Murray

The Very Sleepy Sloth

Jack Tickle

Deep in the jungle,
early in the morning,
the sloth was fast asleep.

But the rest of
the animals were
wide awake.

The cheetah was on
the running machine,
working on his

SPEED.

The elephant was
lifting heavy weights,
working on her

STRENGTH.

The kangaroo was
on the trampoline,
working on her

SPRING

14

The monkey was on the high bars, working on his SWING.

While the sloth stayed
in his hammock,
working on his sleep.

"That sloth is so lazy,"
said Cheetah.

"All he does is lie there!"
agreed Elephant.

"Just dozing in his hammock,"
added Kangaroo.

"Hey, Sloth!" called Monkey.
"We're all working hard here.
Why don't you get up and
do something?"

Sloth slowly opened one eye. "Monkey," he said. "If you're so hard-working, you try lifting Elephant's weights."

"Easy!" said Monkey,
and he tried to lift
the weights.
Elephant giggled as . . .

So Elephant tried to jump on the trampoline. Kangaroo tutted as . . .

21

CRASH!

Elephant fell right through.
"Don't tut at me, Kangaroo!"
said Elephant grumpily.
"Can *you* run like Cheetah?"

So Kangaroo tried
the running machine.
Cheetah chuckled as
Kangaroo landed on . . .

her bottom!

OOOOOOW!

"Cheetah!" said Kangaroo crossly. "If you're so clever, you swing like Monkey."

24

So Cheetah climbed
the high bars and
swung right into . . .

Elephant.

E E E E E EK!

By now, everyone was very hot,
very tired and very, very cross.

"This is useless," they muttered.
"Who caused all this trouble?"

"It wasn't me,"
said Cheetah.
"I was busy running."

"It wasn't me,"
said Kangaroo.
"I was busy bouncing."

"It wasn't me," said Elephant.
"I was busy lifting weights."

"And it wasn't me,"
said Monkey.
"I was busy swinging."

All the animals turned
and looked at . . .

SLOTH!

"Hey, Sloth," they called.
"You started this!"

Sloth turned lazily.
"You must see by now,"
he said. "We were all busy doing
what we do best. Even me!"

The animals thought about it.
"Yes!" they cried. "We're all good at
running or jumping or lifting or
swinging.
But Sloth is the very best at . . .

31

"SNO

OZING!"

"Exactly!" said Sloth.
And with a stretch
and a yawn he fell
fast asleep!

The Smallest Bear

Anne Mangan 🍂 Joanne Moss

Browny was the smallest of all the bears
that lived in the Big Wood. He grew so slowly
that it seemed as if he did not grow at all.
The other young bears would roll him on the
ground and play roly-poly with him and often
they would tease him. "You need to eat more
honey," they laughed, "so that you will
grow bigger."

One day Browny licked Mother Bear's face.
"Yum, you taste nice," he said.
"It must be the honey I ate," said Mother Bear.
"Can you get some for me so that I can grow bigger?"
"No, Browny," said Mother Bear. "Every bear must find his own honey. It is the law of the Big Wood."

Browny ambled off into the Wood. There among
the trees he saw some young bears gathered around
a tree where bees were buzzing.
"Please may I have some of your honey?" he asked
them, "so that I can grow bigger?"
"This is *our* honey," said the big bears. "Go and find
your own!"
And they growled at him and chased him away.

Browny wandered on. Suddenly he came across his Uncle Bruin who had one paw down a hole in a tree-trunk.

"Is that honey in there, Uncle Bruin?" asked Browny. "Please may I have some so that I can grow bigger?"

"No, you may not," replied Uncle Bruin. "Every bear must find his own honey It is the law of the Big Wood. Surely your mother told you that?"

Browny felt sad. Uncle Bruin was usually so kind.
He cheered up, though, when he saw his own friends.
"We're going to look for honey," they called.
"Ooh," said Browny. "I'd like that. I want to grow
bigger, you see. May I come, too?"
"No," said the bears. "You're much too small to
reach the bees' nests."
Browny didn't know what to do. He couldn't grow
bigger if he didn't eat honey, and he couldn't eat
honey because he wasn't big enough to climb trees!

Just at that moment, along came Mr Moose.
He was another friend and he was BIG.
Surely he must know how to grow without
eating honey?
"How can I be as big as you?" asked Browny.
"Some of us are big and some are little," said
Mr Moose and without saying another
word he strode on, with his antlers
touching the branches of the trees.
"Well, that's not much help," said
Browny to himself.

Browny walked on till he reached the lake.
He stood in the water and watched the fish
swimming and splashing. Perhaps *they* would
know how he could grow bigger?
"We only grow as big as we are meant to be,"
said a little fish. "You have to wait to grow."
"But I want to grow *now*!" cried the little bear,
splashing angrily out of the water.

Browny stood under a tree
by the shore and, taking hold
of one of the lowest branches,
he began to stretch himself.
"This will make me
grow a bit bigger.
    Then I'll be able to get
        some honey and grow
            bigger still," he said
                to himself.

He stretched
and he stretched,
but he grew no
bigger at all.

"You do look funny," cried a voice from above his head. "Don't let your friends see you. They will only laugh." It was Squirrel.

What friends? Browny sat up and there, coming towards him, were the big young bears who had growled and chased him earlier in the day.

"They'll think I'm after their honey again," cried
Browny. "Oh, where can I hide?"
"There, over there!" said Squirrel, and Browny
saw some large tree roots arching up over the
ground. He was just small enough to squeeze
between them.
"Aren't you glad now you didn't
grow when you stretched?"
Squirrel called after him.

Browny pushed his way through roots and branches, through briars and tall weeds.
All of a sudden, he came out into a clearing with a lake in the middle.
The sun shone between the trees, and there were butterflies and ladybirds and dragonflies and bees.
And where there are bees, there is *honey*!

The bees kept their honey in a tiny hole
between tree roots, just big enough for
Browny's little paws. He scooped
some out and he ate and . . .

. . . he ate till he could eat no more.
Then he stretched out in a patch of sunlight
and fell fast asleep.

When Browny woke up, he wandered over
to the lake and looked at himself in the water.
He was still as small as ever, but suddenly
it didn't seem to matter any more.
He didn't need to be big to get honey.
He didn't need to be big to be happy.
He was all right, just the way he was!

IT COULD HAVE BEEN WORSE...

by **A.H. Benjamin**

illustrated by **Tim Warnes**

Mouse was on his way back home
after visiting his town cousin,
when . . .

WHOOPS!

. . . he lost his balance
and fell to the ground.

"Ouch!" said Mouse.
"This isn't my lucky
day."

But it could have
been worse!

Mouse picked himself up
and carried on his way.
He came to an open field
and was scurrying across it,
when . . .

CRASH!

... he fell into a hole and disappeared completely.

"Why do things *always*
go wrong for me?"
grumbled Mouse.

But it could have
been worse!

Mouse clambered out of the
hole and was off again.

"I think I'll take a rest," he said.
Mouse had just found a nice
comfy spot, when . . .

OUCH!

... he sat on a thistle
and shot into the air.

"Everything happens
to me!" wailed Mouse
as he pulled some prickles
out of his bottom.

But it could have been worse!

Mouse walked down the hill until he reached a stream. He began to cross it by stepping on the stones, when . . .

SPLASH!

He landed
in the water.

80

"I'll catch my death of cold!" complained Mouse.

But it could have been worse!

Mouse paddled to the edge of the
stream and climbed out of the water.

Shaking himself dry, he was just about
to scramble down a steep bank, when . . .

WHEEE!

He lost his footing and
skidded right to the bottom.

"I'll be black and blue all over," cried Mouse.

But it could have been worse!

Mouse staggered to his feet
and ran all the way home.

"It's been a terrible day," he said to his mum
as she bathed his cuts and bruises. "I fell into
a hole, got wet in the river and -"
"Never mind, Son," said Mum . . .

"It could have been *much* worse!"

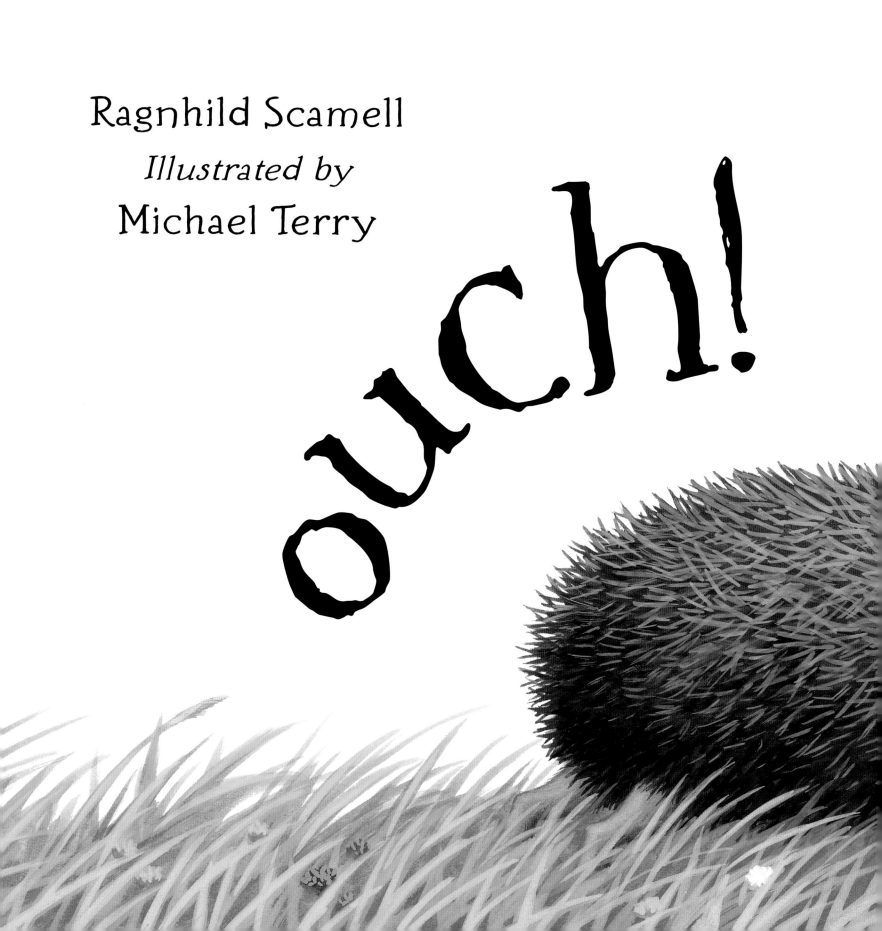

Ragnhild Scamell

Illustrated by

Michael Terry

ouch!

Hedgehog had just finished building her winter nest under the old apple tree. Not too large and not too small. Just right for a nice long winter sleep.

95

Suddenly a juicy
red apple landed
on her back.
   "Ouch!" squeaked
Hedgehog.

Plop!

She curled into a spiny ball, hoping it would fall off. But when she uncurled, the juicy red apple was still there.

Hedgehog tried to squeeze herself and the apple into the beautiful new nest. But could she get in? No. She could not. Not with the apple on her back. The nest was too small.

Oh dear!

Squirrel, scurrying past
with an armful of brown
nuts, stopped to help.

"Stand still. I'll push
the apple off," he said.

And he pushed. And he struggled.

And he heaved. And he tugged . . .

But the juicy red apple stayed where it was.
Worse still, three of Squirrel's brown nuts got
caught in Hedgehog's spines. So now she had
a juicy red apple and three brown nuts on
her back.

"Oh dear!" wailed Hedgehog. "Winter is coming and I can't get into my nest. What will I do?"

"Try rolling on your back," snorted Pig, trotting up. "That'll get rid of it all."

Hedgehog threw herself on the ground. Her little legs paddled in the air as she twisted and wriggled and rolled.

"Has it all gone?" she asked hopefully, scrabbling to her feet.

Pig shook his head. No. The juicy red apple and the three brown nuts were still there. So were a small green pear and a crumpled brown leaf.

"Oh dear," sighed Hedgehog, rolling her eyes.

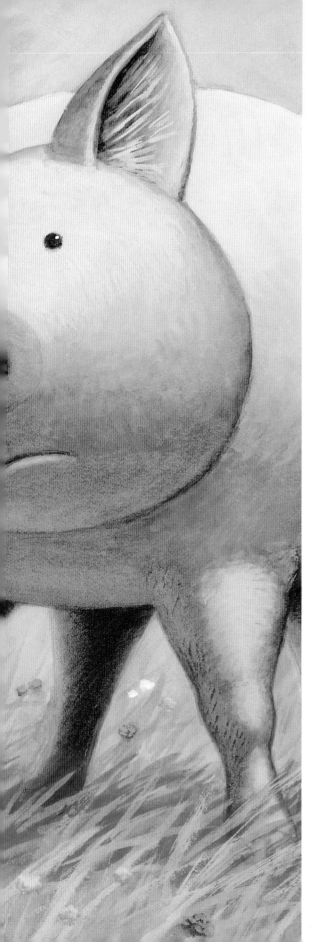

But up in the sky,
sailing towards Hedgehog,
she saw a colourful bit
of card.

"Bother!" she cried.
This way and that she ran,
as fast as she could.

This way and that drifted
the card . . .

. . . and landed right on her back, between the apple and the three brown nuts.

"It's not fair!" cried Hedgehog, who now had a juicy red apple, three brown nuts, a small green pear, a crumpled brown leaf and a colourful bit of card on her back. "I'll never get into my nest!"

Hedgehog pattered to the pond and gazed at her reflection in the water. "Hello, Hedgehog. That's a lot of stuff on your back," croaked Frog. "Hmph! I'm trying to get rid of it," sniffed Hedgehog. "Dive," said Frog. "That will wash it off."

Hedgehog dipped a foot in the murky water, then dived.

Splash! Her friends watched Hedgehog bobbing up and down. The juicy red apple, the three brown nuts, the small green pear, the crumpled brown leaf and the colourful bit of card were all still there.

So was a pink water lily.

"Glug-glug-glug," gurgled Hedgehog as the others heaved her out of the water. She did look funny!

But Hedgehog did not find it funny.

"Stop laughing!" she spluttered and stamped her feet on the ground. "Where am I going to sleep?"

Pig and Squirrel looked worried. So did Frog.

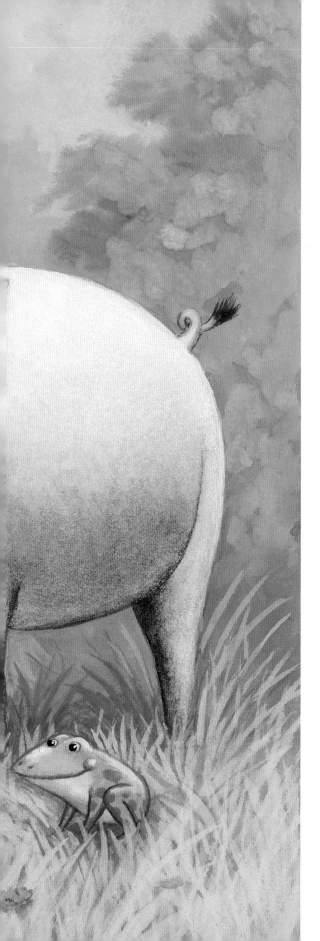

"I do have one
last idea," oinked Pig.
"Squeeze through
that hedge over
there. That'll brush
everything off."
    So Hedgehog
closed her eyes and
squeezed herself
through the thick
leaves. But did it
get everything
off her
back?

No. It did not. It was all still there.
So were four ripe blackberries.
And staring at her, with a look
of great surprise, stood Goat!

"Oooh!" cried Goat. "You've brought LUNCH!"

"Help yourself," said Hedgehog. "Take it all."

"Yippee!" brayed Goat. Then he picked off and ate the juicy red apple, the three brown nuts, the small green pear, the pink water lily and the four ripe blackberries. For pudding, he ate the card. The only thing he left was the crumpled brown leaf. He just couldn't eat any more.

"Hoorah!" cried Hedgehog. She felt as light as a feather. "Thank you, Goat," she said.

Then she ran, as fast as her little legs could carry her, through the gate, past the pond, across the orchard, under the tree and home to her nest.

Hedgehog squeezed into her little nest. It fitted her perfectly. And it was the best nest ever. Outside a cold wind blew another apple off the tree.

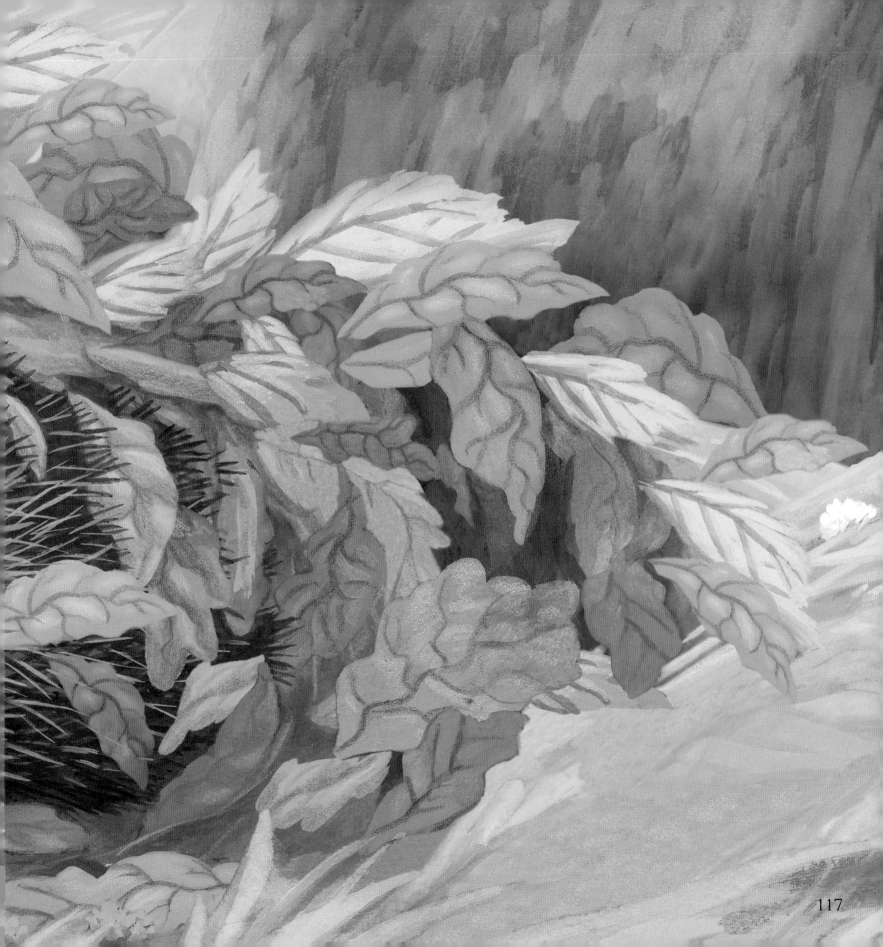